I Spy Fairytales

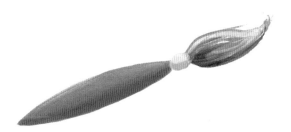

Written by Charlotte Raby
and Emily Guille-Marrett
Illustrated by Deborah Partington

Collins

2

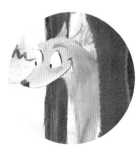

3

4

8

10

12

Match the lost items

 After reading

Letters and Sounds: Phase 1

Word count: 0

Curriculum links: Personal, social and emotional development: Managing feelings and behaviour; Making relationships

Early learning goals: Listening and attention: Listen to stories, accurately anticipating key events and respond to what they hear with relevant comments, questions or actions; Understanding: answer 'how' and 'why' questions about their experiences and in response to stories or events; Reading: demonstrate understanding when talking with others about what they have read

Developing fluency

- Encourage your child to hold the book and to turn the pages.
- Look at the pictures together and ask them to tell each of the fairy tales in their own words.

Phonic practice

- Look at one of the scenes together. Play 'I spy' with your child, putting a lot of emphasis on the initial sound, e.g. on page 3, 'I spy with my little eye, something beginning with "a".' (*axe*). Play this game with the other scenes too, taking turns to spy things in the pictures.

Extending vocabulary

- Look together at the different scenes. Ask your child if they can tell you the names of the items or characters in the little circles at the bottom of each page.
- Ask your child if they can describe them in their own words.

Comprehension

- Ask your child to find the item that each character drops and make sure they notice that the girl picks that item up in the next scene.
- Explore the final scene together and discuss which items have now been returned to their owners. Make sure your child understands that the girl returns to her own world at the end of the book.